Reader in the Sun: Richard Armstrong

PIG PARADE

Gloucester Old Spot: Felicity Bevan

ELM TREE BOOKS · LONDON

The work of the painters shown in this book is available through Portal Gallery, 16a Grafton St, London W.1.

Thanks to the following for permission to quote copyright material in this book:
André Deutsch Ltd for *The Pig* by Ogden Nash, included in *I Wouldn't Have Missed It* (1983)
The estate of the late Sonia Brownell Orwell and Martin Secker & Warburg Ltd for *Animal Farm*
Penguin Books Ltd and Random House Inc for *Hell's Angels* © Hunter Thompson 1966
The Trustees of Wodehouse Trust and Century Hutchinson Ltd for *Pigs Have Wings* and *Pig Hoo-o-o-o-ey* by P.G. Wodehouse

First published in in Great Britain 1985 by Elm Tree Books/Hamish Hamilton Ltd Garden House 57-59 Long Acre London WC2E 9JZ

Copyright © 1985 in the paintings and text written by the artists is the copyright of the artists

© 1985 This collection of paintings and artists' text Beanstalk Books Ltd

Quotes compiled by Jonathon Green

Book design by Patrick Leeson

British Library Cataloguing in Publication Data

Pig parade.
  1. Animal painting and illustration
  2. Swine in art
  758'.3   ND1380
  ISBN 0-241-11692-9

Printed and bound in Spain by Cayfosa Industria Gráfica, Barcelona

Dep. Leg. B. 26.850/85

Pink Pigs and Pink Blossom: Bernard Carter

There warn't nobody at the church, except maybe a hog or two, for there warn't any lock on the door and hogs like a puncheon floor in summertime, because it's cool. If you notice, most folks don't go to church, only when they've got to; but a hog is different.

HUCKLEBERRY FINN: *Mark Twain, 1884*

First Morning Sequence © Kit Williams

Pigs might fly if they had wings.

English proverb

Pigs in a Red Rolls-Royce: Fred Aris

Nothing helps scenery like bacon and eggs.

Mark Twain, 1890

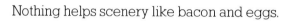

Map Pig: Irvine Peacock

One disadvantage of being a hog is that any moment some bleeding
fool may try to make a silk purse out of your wife's ear.

'Beachcomber' (J.B. Morton)

Lord Holderness Arms: Richard Parker

The pig can hardly be regarded as a classic animal.

RURAL STUDIES: *D.G. Mitchell, 1867*

Commoner's Crown: James Grainger

That pigs can see the wind – in particular the east wind – is a notion
pretty general in the Midlands.

NOTES & QUERIES, 1890

Lily: Christopher Downing

The swine, because it parts the hoof and is cloven-footed but does
not chew the cud is unclean to you; of their flesh you shall not eat,
and their carcass you shall not touch.

LEVITICUS XI, 4

Mer-Pig: Irvine Peacock

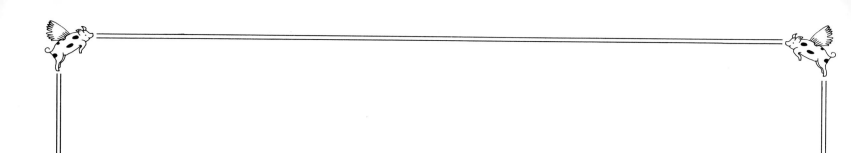

A pig in the parlour is still a pig.

English proverb

Portal Pig R.A.: P. J. Crook

Pig, n. An animal (*Porcus omnivorus*) closely allied to the human race by the splendour and vivacity of its appetite, which, however, is inferior in scope, for it sticks at pig.

THE DEVIL'S DICTIONARY: *Ambrose Bierce, 1881*

Lady and Pig: Fred Aris

Pig. This is the king of unclean beasts; whose empire is most universal, whose qualities are least in question: no pig, no lard, and consequently no cooking, no ham, no sausages, no andouilles, no black puddings and finally no pork-butchers. Ungrateful doctors! you have condemned the pig; he is, as regards indigestion, one of the finest feathers in your cap.

CALENDRIER GASTRONOMIQUE: *Grimod de la Reynière, c. 1800*

This Little Piggy Got Away: David Cheepen

Above all things, keep clean. It is not necessary to be a pig in order
to raise one.

ABOUT FARMING IN ILLINOIS: *R.G. Ingersoll*

Feeding the Pigs: Reg Pepper/Tace Parminter Collection

The boar-pig had drawn nearer to the gate for a closer inspection of the human intruders, and stood champing his jaws and blinking his small red eyes in a manner that was doubtless intended to be disconcerting, and, as far as the Stossens were concerned, thoroughly achieved that result.
'Shoo! Hish! Hish! Shoo!' cried the ladies in chorus.
'If they think they're going to drive him away by reciting lists of the Kings of Israel and Judah they're laying themselves out for disappointment,' observed Matilda...

THE BOAR-PIG: *Saki, 1914*

Royal Inspection: Neil Davenport

Pigs will never play well on the flute, teach them as long as you like.

C.H. Spurgeon, 1880

Pig and Whistle: Barry Castle

One of the first things you learn on a farm is hog-calling. Pigs are temperamental. Omit to call them and they'll starve rather than put on the nose-bag. Call them right, and they will follow you to the ends of the earth with their mouths watering... These calls vary in different parts of America. In Wisconsin, for example, the words 'Poig, Poig, Poig' bring home – in both the literal and the figurative sense – the bacon. In Illinois, I believe they call 'Burp, Burp, Burp', while in Iowa the phrase 'Kus, Kus, Kus' is preferred. Proceeding to Minnesota, we find 'Peega, Peega, Peega' or, alternatively, 'Oink, Oink, Oink', whereas in Milwaukee, so largely inhabited by those of German descent, you will hear the good old Teuton 'Komm Schweine, Komm Schweine'...

PIG HOO-O-O-O-EY!: *P.G. Wodehouse, 1935*

Tennis Champion: Ljiljana Rylands

April 15th, 1778. Brewed a vessel of strong Beer today. My two large
Piggs ... got so amazingly drunk by it, that they were not able to
stand and appeared like dead things almost, and so remained all
night from dinner-time today. I never saw Piggs so drunk in my life. I
slit their ears for them without feeling.
April 16th, 1778. My 2 Piggs are still unable to walk yet, but they are
better than they were yesterday. They tumble about the yard and
can by no means stand at all steady yet. In the evening my 2 Piggs
were tolerably sober.

DIARY OF A COUNTRY PARSON: *James Woodforde*

Swinging Pig: Janice Thompson

Lawsuit: a machine which you go into as a pig and come out as a
sausage.

THE DEVIL'S DICTIONARY: *Ambrose Bierce, 1911*

The Secret of Mr Apollinaire: James McNaught

THE LITTLE SECRET OF APOLLINAIRE

They say if pigs fly they always go with their tails forward.

C.H. Spurgeon, 1880

Celebes Island Pig: Lizzie Riches

E·R

'If you're going to turn into a pig, my dear,' said Alice seriously, 'I'll have nothing more to do with you. Mind now!' The poor little thing sobbed again (or grunted, it was impossible to say which), and they went on for some while in silence… This time there could be no mistake about it: it was neither more nor less than a pig and she felt it would be quite absurd for her to carry it any further.
So she set the little creature down… 'If it had grown up,' she said to herself, 'it would have made a dreadfully ugly child: but it makes rather a handsome pig, I think.' And she began thinking over other children she knew, who might do very well as pigs… 'if only one knew the right way to change them –'

ALICE'S ADVENTURES IN WONDERLAND: *Lewis Carroll, 1865*

Pig Traveller: Rosemary Fawcett

The pig has lived only to eat, he eats only to die… He eats everything his gluttonous snout touches, he will be eaten completely… he eats all the time, he will be eaten all the time… The pig is nothing but an enormous dish which walks while waiting to be served… In a sort of photograph of his future destiny, everything announces that he will be eaten, but eaten in such a fashion that there will remain of him not the smallest bone, not a hair, not an atom.

LETTRES GOURMANDES: *Charles Monselet, 1874*

Dog and Bacon: Janice Thompson

Had I a sucking-pig,
Ere he had grown as big
Even as a pint bottle or a rolling-pin,
He should have learned to be
Faithful and true to thee,
Yes, his first squeak should be
'Comrade Napoleon!'

ANIMAL FARM: *George Orwell, 1945*

Mistletoe Oak © Kit Williams

Little pigs eat big potatoes.

Irish proverb

Pigments of the Imagination: James Grainger

The Empress lived in a bijou residence not far from the kitchen garden, and when Lord Emsworth arrived at her boudoir she was engaged, as pretty nearly always when you dropped in on her, in hoisting into her vast interior those fifty-seven thousand and eight hundred calories on which Whiffle insists. Monica Simmons, the pig girl, had done her well in the way of barley meal, maize meal, linseed meal, potatoes and separated buttermilk, and she was digging in and getting hers in a manner calculated to inspire the brightest confidence in the bosoms of her friends and admirers.

PIGS HAVE WINGS: *P.G. Wodehouse, 1952*

Olympia: Mark Copeland

The pig, if I am not mistaken,
Supplies us sausage, ham and bacon.
Let others say his heart is big –
I call it stupid of the pig.

THE PIG: *Ogden Nash*

Tattooed Pig: Fergus Hall

In the argot of the cycle world, a Harley is a 'hog' and the outlaw bike is a 'chopped hog'. Basically it is the same machine all motorcycle cops use, but the police bike is an accessory-loaded elephant compared to the lean, customized dynamos the Hell's Angels ride. The resemblance is about the same as that of a factory-equipped Cadillac to a dragster's stripped-down essence of the same car.

HELL'S ANGELS: *Hunter S. Thompson, 1966*

Road Hog: Maggie Oliver

Poets and pigs are not appreciated until they are dead.

Italian proverb

Harlequin Pig: Peter Lawman

ARTISTS' NOTES

Reader in the Sun: Richard Armstrong
This painting began when I saw a workman sitting in his wheelbarrow and basking in the sunshine. He was absorbed in the sort of newspaper that does not make great demands on the intellect in a brief lunch break. The title came readily to mind and I knew that I had the idea for a painting, but as it stood it was too ordinary ... It was as I photographed him and saw that he was too mesmerised by the page three pin-up to notice me that the cliché 'Male Chauvinist Pig' came to mind. Suddenly the image of a pig in the barrow seemed very satisfactory with its echo of the old (but good) joke and the opportunity of creating a 'Page three' pig.

Gloucester Old Spot: Felicity Bevan
The simple sheep is most suited to these bleak northern hills; it will graze contentedly in the most inhospitable of climes. The pig, however, poses merely for our benefit and would prefer a therapeutic mud bath or steaming sty. Like many a captive animal he has an air of resignation and thinks, no doubt, a very superior thought.

Pink Pigs and Pink Blossom: Bernard Carter
One day when we were rowing on the Thames near Witney we saw some pigs who came to chat with us. The boar asked me the meaning of the phrase 'Male Chauvinist Pig' (which he'd heard bandied about between the farmer and his wife) and he asked if I was one. I replied, 'No' and he said he thought *he* was, and looked rather pleased!

First Morning Sequence © Kit Williams
Originally one of a pair of paintings designed to be hung on facing walls of a room, each picture looking at the other. This causes space between to be subtly altered and a viewer standing there feels himself to be an intruder.

As with all grand schemes, circumstances change events. The pictures were sold separately and now hang on walls in different continents, making all who stand before them innocent intruders.

Pigs in a Red Rolls-Royce: Fred Aris
There isn't any deep hidden meaning in this – I just wanted to do an amusing painting. The idea of a Rolls-Royce stuffed full of squealing pigs and driven by a rather pompous-looking chauffeur appealed to my sense of the ridiculous. I also had a feeling of nostalgia for the days when motor cars were upright and elegant and were not designed for the sole purpose of tearing down the motorway at 70mph.

Map Pig: Irvine Peacock
This carefree young boar is performing the intricate 'Coronation Dance'. The red ribbon indicates that he is unmarried while the map shows the precise location of his treasure.

Lord Holderness Arms: Richard Parker
This watercolour is based on an allegorical bookplate I engraved to mark the creation of Rt. Hon. Richard Wood to be Baron Holderness. It incorporates elements of his new armorial bearings and family history.

The Indian arches represent his father the Earl of Halifax's time as Viceroy of India. The wild boar is one of the supporters of the arms where it is shown holding an anchor – this, along with the distant sailing ship, represents a seafaring ancestor of his wife, who explored the Polar regions. The boar lies on a cushion bearing the motto 'I Still Like My Choice' by which stands a military bearskin; this comes from the other armorial supporter and represents Lord Holderness's position as Hon. Colonel 4th (Volunteer) Battalion Royal Green Jackets.

Commoner's Crown: James Grainger
Maytime has always been a season for great rejoicing. Not only are the hardships of winter over but, more importantly, the last crops of the revolting Brussels sprout have been harvested and eaten. Cabbage-hating natives of Margate celebrate Maytime by the crowning of a randomly selected commoner. (According to an ancient Thanet manuscript a commoner is 'One who hath habit of dropping his H's'.)

Best hunting grounds for coronation victims are outside the guest houses of gentlemen attending a coinciding Pork Salesmen Conference. These rogues are often overhead saying 'I'm staying in an 'otel' and are immediately bagged. After much persuasive talk they are dragged, kicking, by the local vicar to the ceremonial grounds.

The chosen one is seated on the back of a pig and a crown of rhubarb is placed upon his head. Dancing and celebrations go on late into the night while the new May King is subdued by the enforced sniffing of May blossom.

The use of a pig as a throne comes from pre-refrigeration times, when from May (the first month in the year without an 'R') flesh of pigs became sacred and could not be eaten. It was in fact during a crowning ceremony that top pork salesman, Commander Corriander Jones invented his famous calendar with an 'R' in every month in an attempt to boost summer pork sales.

Lily: Christopher Downing
As a small boy in Shropshire I remember a sow from the farm opposite decided to inspect our garden, with a view to having her litter there. With the memory of this in mind I painted Lily roaming paths of wild flower scents among fields of oil-seed rape and Suffolk thatch.

Merpig: Irvine Peacock
Almost forgotten now, the Merpig was first described in the infamous 'Song of the Loathsome Stone'. This now unobtainable pamphlet caused something of a stir when published in 1937 by the self-styled Rev. William J. Buckworth. So much so that until the onset of hostilities in 1939 busloads of morbid sightseers arrived daily to view the so-called 'tombs' which at that time were still visible at low tide. Dismissed today as the 'ravings of a brilliant but diseased mind' it is generally accepted that the controversial poems were written by Duckworth himself shortly before his mysterious disappearance. Certainly the ill-fated expedition from the American Museum of Natural History could throw little light on the matter and frankly neither this painting nor the bizarre objects uncovered with it give any cause for disagreeing with the initial committee of enquiry.

Portal Pig R.A.: P.J. Crook
I suspect that any pig who frequents the Portal Gallery must be of the painting breed. An immaculate dresser, he designs and stitches his own clothes, wearing them with great style. Ambitious and painstaking, he looks with great reverence at the grand building just around the corner in Piccadilly that houses the works of so many of his past and present heroes – he longs to be amongst them.

Lady and Pig: Fred Aris
When I painted this 'pig' painting I wanted it to be a happy painting. I also wanted to convey a pig as a friend with a distinct character and individual personality – not just Sunday breakfast or covered in parsley sauce.

This Little Piggy Got Away: David Cheepen

While it has become fashionable recently to care about the survival of whole species, the fate of individual creatures (other than certain well-known zoo animals or valuable racehorses) has excited less media concern.

So as to express – as a vegetarian – my own awareness of the value of every single living creature, I decided in this picture to produce a 'head-and-shoulders' portrait, so as to emphasise the individuality of my subject.

My pig, as the painting's title implies, is an escapee.

Set in a spacious landscape, which symbolises his new-found freedom, he regards the viewer with an indignant, knowing stare that reveals considerable intelligence and dignity.

Feeding the Pigs: Reg Pepper

I rather doubt if a pig can shout,
But if he could
He'd call for green grass and a shaded wood.

Royal Inspection: Neil Davenport

When Neil Davenport was staying with us in Somerset in 1981 he saw a book by our neighbour Ralph Whitlock called *Royal Farmers* and was much tickled by a photograph of a pig hanging over its sty door at Windsor to shake hooves with a somewhat embarrassed George VI. He decided this was just the swine for the Portal Pig Show.

(Sadly Neil Davenport died in 1984 and this was written by Sally Pasmore, a life-long friend.)

Pig and Whistle: Barry Castle

I daydreamed I could execute
harmoniously on the flute;
that I was able to enthrall
enthusiasts in a concert hall;
then woke to find all as before
a pig my only auditor.
But music is a force that mellows
even most unlikely fellows –
the pig appeared to be asleep
but as I prayed I saw him weep.

Tennis Champion: Ljiljana Rylands

At the time this picture was made I decided to give the pig an air of haughty and ostentatious triumph – I thought this would be an amusing interpretation of a 'pig' theme. He stands raised on a rostrum in a pretentious pose. He is stitched simply but carefully in embroidered cottons on canvas; the entire image measures four inches by three inches.

Swinging Pig: Janice Thompson

Sure as a pig flies
Lazing in the sun,
Sty needs a clean-up
Dog needs a run.
Must watch out for the boss man's gun,
He's always out to spoil my fun.

The Secret of Mr Apollinaire: James McNaught

Guillaume Apollinaire, poet and art critic, sat for several portrait drawings by Picasso in 1916, while in Paris convalescing from a war wound. But in the prevailing pessimism of Paris, Apollinaire grew restless and this mood moved him to have his portrait painted by me as 'The Last Great Pig Magician'.

Celebes Island Pig: Lizzie Riches

The hairless pig of the Celebes – the Babirussa – has extraordinarily long and curved upper and lower canine teeth. Native legend has it that the pigs hang suspended by their curved teeth in trees at night in order to sleep. In fact the tusks have no function at all and even sometimes kill the pigs by growing into the brain.

Pig Traveller: Rosemary Fawcett

When we are young, adventures always begin with a spotted handkerchief and stick and a farewell note. Nothing changes. This happy pig is leaving the world of adults forever…

Dog and Bacon: Janice Thompson

The Dog and Bacon Inn in Horsham, Sussex, was originally The Dog and Beacon, but the name changed over the years because of the sound of the Sussex accent. Also, many small farmers in Sussex were pig-breeders.

The Sussex Downs near Horsham were the site of one of the ancient beacons that were lit around the British Isles to send messages to the population about war, coronations, etc. These beacons were lit again on the night before the wedding of the Prince and Princess of Wales.

Mistletoe Oak © Kit Williams

This picture, with its elaborate frame, describes the ever-changing state of matter in the universe.

The parasitic mistletoe and the acorn-eating pigs feed freely from the oak tree, whilst the tree takes its nourishment from the earth and, by inference, from the pigs. Valuable minerals and salts are constantly being passed on from one life form to another, ever-changing but never destroyed.

The Druids chose the oak as a symbol of life and mistletoe growing on an oak was deemed especially sacred.

Pigments of the Imagination: James Grainger

To the average chap a full moon poses little threat to daily routine. For some, however, its effects result in uncontrollable urges and desires fulfilled only by performing bizarre rituals. One such ceremony is the 'Walthamstow Pig Stalk' where an imaginary multi-coloured pig is pursued using acorns picked by the village idiot, as bait. The traditional headgear for the event is a crown crafted from sheets of Public Lavatory paper.

It is said that, should the pig ever be sighted, the spotter's inner self will leap screaming over the moon wearing ill-fitting boots borrowed from a postman.

Olympia: Mark Copeland

I thought I would do a send-up of Manet's painting of the same name: after all, why shouldn't a pig have her admirers too?

Tattooed Pig: Fergus Hall

Pigs seems to be sensible, intelligent creatures and we humans keep them in such dirty conditions and then hold our noses. My pig wants to be a dandy and as it would be silly to dress him up, he just had to be tattooed. Pigs can be beautiful with a little encouragement.

Road Hog: Maggie Oliver

When I was invited to paint a picture for Portal's 1982 Christmas Pig Exhibition my whole family joined forces to think of an idea for me to work on. This painting was prompted by my nephew, who said that there was a saying in Germany which, loosely translated, meant 'driving like a wild pig' from which the expression 'Road Hog' was obviously derived.

Harlequin Pig: Peter Lawman

The idea for this picture came to me while I was travelling home on a westbound coach along the M4. So it is a travelling picture – perhaps a honeymoon journey – the wayfaring pig has quite a spring in his step.

For the figures, I had in mind the kind of imagery found in the Tarot, specifically 'The Fool'

and 'The High Priestess'. The small pig in the stern of the ship was included as an amusing addition to invite speculation about the relationship between the main figures.

The influence of fairy tales was so strong that I contemplated 'Fairy Tale' as a title, but it didn't seem quite right somehow. Then Jess of the Portal Gallery suggested 'Harlequin Pig', which I think suits it well.

Over the Hill: Avril Lydiate

As pigs are usually seen in muddy sties and farmyards I thought it would be interesting to paint my pig in a pastoral setting. I wanted the painting to have an air of melancholy about it, which is why I chose this title. The pig's rear view, slumped shoulders and general demeanour suggest to me a feeling of opportunities passed by, a worldweariness.

Over the Hill: Avril Lydiate

Reader in the Sun: Richard Armstrong